480   41253

AMBER ON THE MOUNTAIN

Tony Johnston · Paintings by Robert Duncan

Dial Books for Young Readers *New York*

Published by Dial Books for Young Readers
A Division of Penguin Books USA Inc.
375 Hudson Street
New York, New York 10014

Designed by Nancy R. Leo
Printed in Hong Kong
First Edition
1 3 5 7 9 10 8 6 4 2

Library of Congress Cataloging in Publication Data
Johnston, Tony.
Amber on the mountain / by Tony Johnston ; paintings by Robert Duncan. — 1st ed.
p.   cm.
Summary: Isolated on her mountain, Amber meets and befriends a girl from the city
who gives her the determination to learn to read and write.
ISBN 0-8037-1219-7. — ISBN 0-8037-1220-0 (lib. bdg.)
[1. Literacy — Fiction. 2. Friendship — Fiction. 3. Mountain life — Fiction.]
I. Duncan, Robert, ill. II. Title.
PZ7.J6478Am 1994   [E] — dc20   93-16292   CIP   AC

*The full-color artwork for each painting is oil on canvas. It was color-separated
and reproduced as red, blue, yellow, and black halftones.*

For Marilyn Carpenter, Betsy Crane, Candace Lynch,
and Doris Peters — great ladies of literacy, great friends
T.J.

With love for Josh, Mandy, Christian, Brianne, Braden, and Cullen
R.D.

You are gone away, away.
Clouds come flinging down
the rain.
Comes your letter.
You are here, singing, with me
once again.

— *Tony Johnston*

AMBER lived on a mountain so high, it poked through the clouds like a needle stuck in down. Trees bristled on it like porcupine quills. And the air made you giddy—it was that clear. Still, for all that soaring beauty, Amber was lonesome. For mountain people lived scattered far from one another.

Once a man came on horseback to teach the people to read and write. How Amber longed to read and write! Books would be good company. But mountain life was too hard for the man. He left his supplies behind and skedaddled before winter came.

One day another man came with a crew to build a road. His wife and daughter, Anna, came too.

Amber's Granny Cotton told the man straight out, "You can't build a road here. Folks will roll clean off it, like walking up a wall."

But the man said, "You can do almost anything you fix your mind on."

He fixed his mind on building that road.

Now Amber had seen Anna with her family, inching their way up the mountain. She wanted to be friends.

But Amber was shy.

I will say "hey" to her when the time is right, Amber thought.

Meanwhile, she watched Anna, biding her time.

One day Amber was watching. Anna lay flopped on her stomach in a meadow, reading a book. The sky was streaked with morning. The air was warm. The grass hummed with bees.

Suddenly, up jumped Anna shouting, *"Once upon a time—"* and hopping around, crazy as a doodlebug.

Amber decided the time was right to say "hey."

"Hey!" she called. "Are you crazy?"

"Sure!" Anna called back. "Crazy with spring! Hey, yourself!"

"What are you shouting?" asked Amber.

"A story from my book. About a princess spinning gold."

"Might I hold it?" Amber asked.

"Sure."

Amber took the book as if it were a fine and breakable cup. She examined the pages.

"This tells of a princess—truly?" she asked.

"Yep. Want to read it?"

"I don't know how," Amber said. "There's no school hereabouts."

"I forgot," said Anna.

She stared at Amber. A stubborn look came into her eyes.

Amber giggled. "You look like our mule, Rockhead. When old Rockhead looks balkity, he's up to something sure."

"Well, I *am* up to something," said Anna. "Daddy says you can do almost anything you fix your mind on. I've just fixed mine on teaching you to read!"

"For real and true?" cried Amber.

"For real and true."

Anna began shouting from the book again. Amber joined in. Then they twirled through the grass, crazy as *two* doodlebugs.

After that, Anna and Amber stuck to each other like burrs.

When Amber did her chores, Anna helped. She learned to slop the pigs, milk the goat, and gather eggs. When Granny Cotton needed "young eyes" to help with her quilting, the girls sat on either side of her, poking little silver needles in and out, in and out.

Whatever else they did, every day they practiced reading.

Learning to read was like walking up a wall. Amber kept rolling off.

"These marks are like the chicken tracks in our yard," she moaned. "I know for a fact chickens don't write notes to each other. Are you certain sure these letters mean something?"

"Certain sure." Anna smiled.

Sometimes Amber read a few words. Then she stumbled. Sometimes she forgot the words and had to start all over. She was so eager, she hurried and tangled the words like quilting thread.

"Drat!" Amber grumbled. "I plain can't do this!"

"You *can*," said Anna. "Just pretend you're old Rockhead. Set your whole self to the task."

Amber stiffened up mulish as could be.

Anna howled with delight. "Now *that* is the face of a reader!"

And one day — one very fine day — Amber took the book and read, "And he stamped his foot through the floor and was never seen again. The end."

"You did it!" hooted Anna. "You read all by yourself!"

"I read! I read! I READ!"

The girls marched around, stomping their feet like Rumpelstiltskin.

Suddenly Anna stopped. She stared at Amber.

"Just what notion have you *now,* Miss Rockhead?" Amber asked.

"Now I've fixed my mind on teaching you to write!" said Anna.

But that was not to be. The road was finished. Anna and her family were going home.

When the day of parting came, each gave the other a gift. Anna gave Amber her book of fairy tales. Amber gave Anna a little clay mule.

Then Amber watched her friend down the mountain till she melted into blue mountain mist.

Months passed. Mountain people went down the road and learned the ease of city ways. City people came up the road and learned the beauty of mountain ways. And funny thing — not one solitary soul rolled off that road.

From time to time up on the mountain, Amber got a letter from Anna. Then she glowed with happiness. Anna's words set them side by side again. But Amber was sad too. She missed her friend. And she could not tell her so.

But one day she got a notion. A wonderful, rockheaded notion.

"Attention! Attention!" she announced to the chickens. "I've fixed my mind on learning to write. Soon I'll send Anna a letter frilly as lace. And she'll faint right to the floor!"

The chickens paid no attention. Amber didn't care. She ran straight to Granny Cotton, jibbering her news out before she stopped.

Granny chuckled. "Child, child, you're peltering me with words, thick as spring rain. I feel drenched."

Granny was so pleased, she gave Amber the paper and pencils left behind by the teacher long ago.

Whenever she could squeeze in time, Amber took her book and tried to copy the words.

If I can read 'em, I can copy 'em, she thought.

At first they looked squat and squashed.

"My letters are lopsided as a herd of one-horned cows," she groaned.

Amber kept working.

When it snowed and the world outside was muffled in white, she huddled under a quilt so only her hands poked out. Cold and stiff, she formed her letters.

When clouds like grey geese flocked in the sky and rain glazed the land, Amber shivered. But she kept working.

Her tongue curled to her upper lip in concentration, like a lizard stalking a bug. She squeezed her pencil nearly to splinters. Her fingers hurt. Still, she kept working.

And one day — one very fine day — Amber sent a letter to Anna.

> Dear Anna,
> I am a rockhead to. I fixed my mind on riting. I teached myself to rite sos I can rite you. I hop you faynt to the flor.
> Love from yer frend Amber

Soon a letter came back.

Dear Rockhead,

    Your letter made me faint right <u>through</u> the floor, like you-know-who! It made me happy. You are not far away anymore.

                          Love from your friend,

                              Anna